ISBN-9781973338260

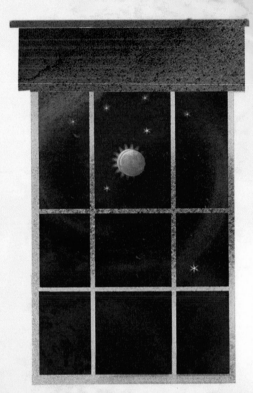

For Ben, my Dooka Dook

Ben was dreaming when he woke to his rooster greeting the sun.

Cock-A-Doodle-Do!

"Hang on Big Red, I'll be right there."

Ben skipped breakfast, running straight to his hen yard to see what all the fuss was about.

Big Red had run off to chase away an uninvited guest.

One of his hens was missing!

Ben finds Cozette several feet from the safety of the coop. She's scratching at the ground near the edge of the forest surrounding the hen yard.

"What have you found Cozette?"

"It's a Super Suit!"

"If only I could really fly!"

Ben says with excitement as he pretends to be super

A book drops from the cape of Ben's suit. On the first page, he finds instructions.

To fly, take three steps and jump toward the sky.

You must return home before the sun sets. If you lose the race, you'll be super for just one day.

Ben takes three steps and jumps toward the sky to chase the sun.

"I'm flying, look at me, I'm flying!"

You in the sky, hear my plea.
I'm away from my family,
I belong in the sea.

"I'll be back, don't you see?
I'll be back to set you free."

These amazing creatures belong in their natural habitat.

The sea!

With his super vision, Ben sees a lonely tiger. His home has been turned to iron and stone.

"I'll be back, don't you see? I'll be back to set you free."

Big cats like to roam free. They like the mountains and forests. Some, like the Sumatran tiger, are found hunting in swamps!

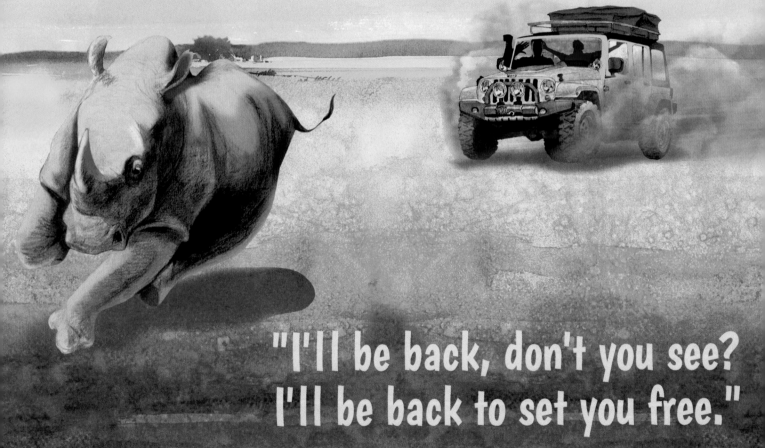

These ancient creatures were once the largest animals on land. Their ancestors date back 50 million years!

Just as the sun is within
Ben's reach, he sees a
turtle struggling for the beach.

"I'll be back, don't you see?

I'll be back
to set you free."

Sea turtles have lived on our planet and traveled the Earth's seas for the last 100 million years. They are vital for the health of sea beds and coral reefs.

Ben nearly catches the sun when he looks down and sees a forest in despair. Thousands of tiny voices call for his help.

"I can't stop now, I've come too far. Look to the sky, I can beat this star!"

Rainforests are home to half of the planet's plant and animal species and are winter homes to many birds.

They are some of the most beautiful places on Earth.

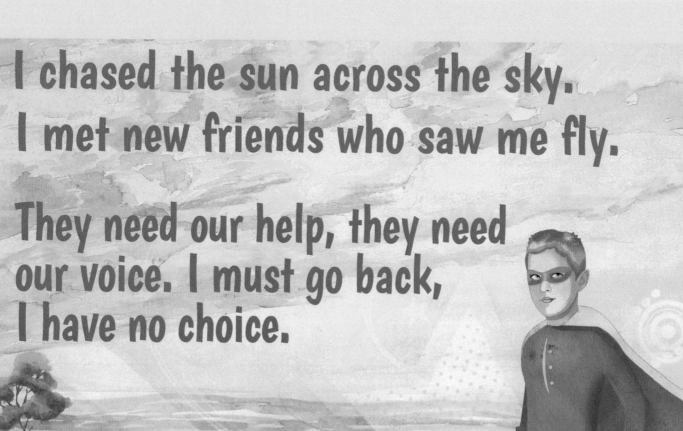

I chased the sun across the sky.
I met new friends who saw me fly.

They need our help, they need
our voice. I must go back,
I have no choice.

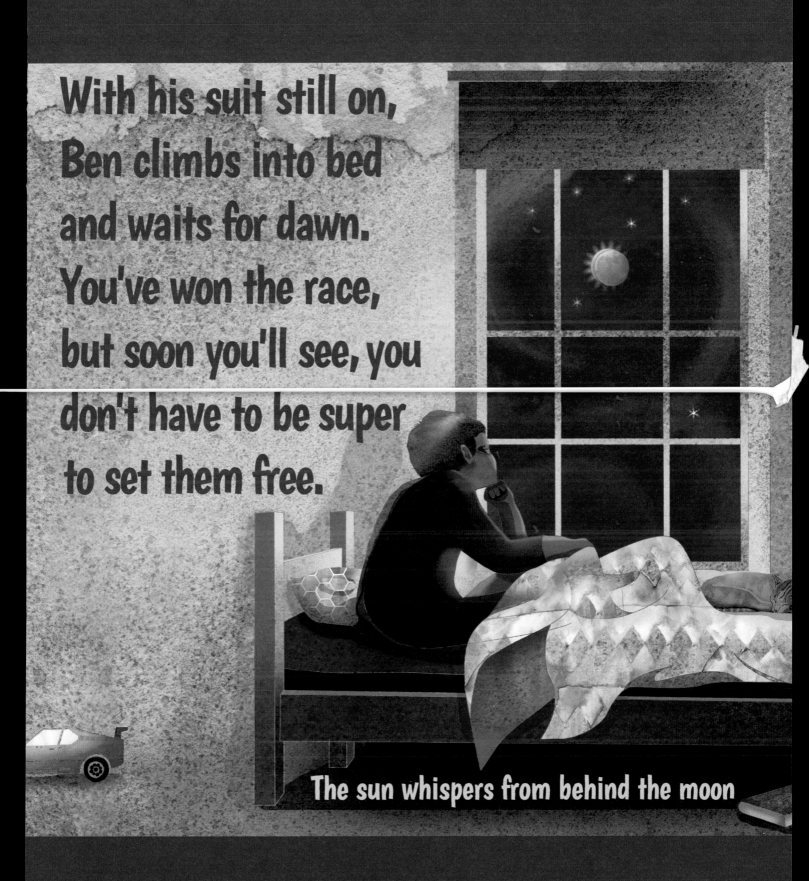

With his suit still on,
Ben climbs into bed
and waits for dawn.
You've won the race,
but soon you'll see, you
don't have to be super
to set them free.

The sun whispers from behind the moon

Cock-A-Doodle-Do!

Was it all just a dream?

Someone truly SUPER once said-

"Only if we understand, will we care. Only if we care, will we help. Only if we help shall all be saved. Every individual matters. Every individual has a role to play. Every individual makes a difference. The least I can do is speak out for those who cannot speak for themselves".

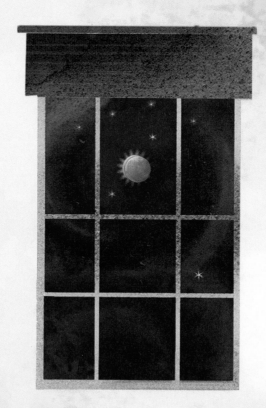

The End